P9-DMX-084

JIN WOO

For Suzanne and Bruce, Jin Woo's parents.
And, of course, for Jin Woo.
Special thanks to Nancy J. Johnson,
who introduced us.
—E.B.

For my mom, and for adoptive families
who have selflessly dedicated their hearts
and homes to adoptees like me.
—C.S.

Clarion Books
a Houghton Mifflin Company imprint
215 Park Avenue South, New York, NY 10003

The illustrations were executed in watercolor.
The text was set in 16-point Centaur.
Book design by Kimi Weart.

www.houghtonmifflinbooks.com
Printed in U.S.A.

Library of Congress Cataloging-in-Publication Data

Bunting, Eve, 1928–
Jin Woo / by Eve Bunting; illustrated by Chris K. Soentpiet.
p. cm.
Summary: Davey is dubious about having a new adopted brother
from Korea, but when he finds out that his parents still love him,
he decides that having a baby brother will be fine.
ISBN 0-395-93872-4
[1. Adoption—Fiction. 2. Brothers—Fiction. 3. Korean Americans—Fiction.]
I. Soentpiet, Chris K., ill. Title.
PZ7.B91527 Ji 2001 [E]—dc21 00-038408

BVG 10 9 8 7 6 5 4 3

Jin Woo

by Eve Bunting
Illustrated by
Chris Soentpiet

Clarion Books • New York

When we get the phone call, Mom and Dad cry.

Mom hugs me. "He's coming, David. I'm so happy!"

I'm happy, too. I think.

"He's coming when?" I ask.

"Tomorrow. Early." Mom runs to Dad and they hold each other. They spread their arms wide so they can hold me, too.

"I can hardly wait," Mom says.

I can wait. I could wait longer.

They'd told me they were trying to get another baby. One from a different country who needed parents. They asked me how I would feel about that.

"OK," I'd said. Kind of OK. I thought it wouldn't happen. But it's happening.

Last week we painted the nursery pale yellow, with the ceiling blue as the summer sky. We go in now to look at it.

There's the crib that used to be mine before I got my big-boy bed. There's the chair where Mom sat to rock me. His baby clothes are on it, folded and ready.

Dad gets the photo that has been stuck on the refrigerator for weeks and gives it to Mom. She holds it against her cheek. "Precious baby!" she whispers.

We go out to dinner to celebrate. Mom tells the waiter about the baby. "He's coming from Korea," she says. "That's why we came to a Korean restaurant tonight. His name is Jin Woo." She shows him the photograph.

She and Dad don't eat much.

"Too excited," Mom says.

I drink my milk. Were they this excited when they adopted me?

When we're leaving, the lady at the desk says, "Bring that baby in. We'll serve him kimchi."

Dad laughs. "Pickled vegetables!" he says. "Not till he has teeth."

Later, when they tuck me into bed, we say prayers. We ask that Jin Woo will be brought to us safely. Dad asks for help so they will be good parents to him.

"You will," I say. "You are the best."

I lie in bed and think about Jin Woo. I watch the rubber ducks that dangle above my bed dive and bob beneath my ceiling. When I was a baby, they hung over my crib. I love my ducks. If I'm mixed up or scared about something, I watch them. They have such happy faces. They make me feel better. Mom and Dad are talking in the living room, and I know it's about the new baby who's coming.

"Good night, ducks," I say and I try not to cry. I tell myself it will be all right.

It's still dark in the morning when they wake me. They're already dressed.

I put on my clothes as slowly as I can.

"Hurry, sweetheart," Mom calls. "Do you need help?"

"No," I mutter.

My old car seat is belted in the back of the car. It's empty now, but he'll be in it coming back. I look out of the car window and see only me in the dark glass.

The airport is almost empty.

"It's because it's so early," Dad says.

He has brought a Thermos of coffee for them and apple juice for me. There's a bag of muffins. And a bottle for Jin Woo.

We wait and wait. Mom keeps saying, "Where's that plane? What if he isn't on it?" And Dad takes her hand and holds it and strokes it.

And then he shouts, "Here it comes!"

We run to the big glass window.

It's the most awesome plane I've ever seen. It comes gliding down the runway like a gigantic pterodactyl.

"Cool!" I whisper, happy for a minute, forgetting that the new baby's inside.

The plane stops.

The woman carrying the baby is the last to come off. He's wrapped in a blue blanket.

We're separated from the passengers by a wall of glass, but we can watch as they go down a long escalator. They disappear through a door at the bottom.

RL

Mom clutches at Dad's arm. "Where has she taken him?" she whispers.

"They have to go through customs, sweetheart," Dad says. "They'll be back."

It's not long till they come out and ride the escalator up again.

The woman sees us watching and she smiles. She holds the baby up to the glass.

I see a little round face. He doesn't look like his picture.

"I don't think that's the right one," I say, hoping. Maybe they'll send him back.

Dad grins. "He's changed since the photo. He's five months old now."

Then the lady frees one of his arms from the blanket and makes him wave to us.

We wave back. Mom is sobbing out loud. They are leaning so close to the glass that it's getting blurry with their breaths.

My stomach hurts.

We have to wait some more to sign papers, and then the woman gives the blue bundle to Mom.

"Here he is," she says. She looks sad, as if she doesn't want to give him up. "He was so good on the plane. I escort a lot of babies and this one is exceptional."

"Do you hear that?" Mom coos to Jin Woo. "Oh, you are so exceptional!" She kisses his fat little cheek.

"His name means Happy Jewel," the woman says. "And here." She gives Dad a box. "This is his *hanbok* to wear on his first birthday. It is traditional."

"What's a hanbok?" I wonder.

"We'll see that he knows about it, and all his traditions," Dad says.

The woman puts a small gold ring in Dad's hand. "This is the ring he wore on his hundredth day. We celebrated having him with us for all that time."

"Will you keep it for him, David?" Dad asks me.

"Sure." I put it in my pocket.

Dad smiles. "Good job!"

Mom gives Jin Woo to him and he gets all blurry eyed. Then she says, "If you sit down, Davey, you can hold him."

I sit down and Dad puts him in my lap.

"Hi." I peer into Jin Woo's face. "You're pretty heavy for a little kid!"

On the way home he is in the car seat and I am beside him. I take one of his hands and play This Little Piggy Went to Market, even though these are fingers, not toes.

He gives a funny, gurgling laugh.

"Wow, Davey! His first laugh since he came. And it's all for you," Mom says.

I grin. "Cool!" And I do the piggy thing again.

All the neighbors come out to *ooh* and *aah* over Jin Woo.

Mrs. Jones-Christopher from next door says, "Hi, Davey! There's almost as much hoopla today as there was when your parents brought you home. That was quite an event." She points. "Your father stood on those steps and belted out 'God Bless America.'"

I'm shocked. "My dad?"

"Yep. And he's the worst singer I ever heard."

I can tell I'm smiling, and I'm definitely feeling better. Partly it's because of the piggy thing.

In the nursery, Mom changes Jin Woo's diaper. He doesn't cry or fuss.

"What a happy baby," Mom says.

She and Dad say, "Look at his darling chubby legs! Look at that chubby little belly!"

He's chubby, that's for sure.

We take turns kissing his chubby little belly. He smells nice.

Then Mom says the baby must be tired after his long trip, so she lays him in his crib.

Dad and I open the box. Inside are tiny satin pants and a bright blue jacket with striped sleeves.

Mom smiles, "Oh, he's going to look so cute."

She sits in the rocking chair and takes a letter from her pocket. "Davey. This letter is from Jin Woo to you."

I look at the envelope. "Naw. He can't write yet."

"Would you like me to read it to you? Would you like to sit on my lap?"

I nod and Dad comes to sit beside us, cross-legged on the floor.

"Dear David," Mom reads.

"It's going to be scary for me for a while. Everything will be so different. I'm glad I have you to help me. Mom and Dad told me how much they love you. And how much they will love me. They say they have so much love inside of them that what they give to me won't take any away from you."

I turn to look at Mom. "Really truly?"

"Really truly. That's the way love is." She looks at the letter again. "Jin Woo says you and he will have fun together."

"But he couldn't have written this. He's just a baby."

"I helped him because I knew what was in his heart," Mom says. "Just the way I know what's in yours."

"You do?"

"I do." She puts her cheek against mine.

I hope she doesn't know what was in my heart before. She can look now if she likes because what is in there is better.

I wiggle off her lap and the three of us go across and stand around the crib.

Jin Woo's awake, watching the sun shadows on the ceiling.

Is he scared now? Is he unhappy? I don't know about babies.

I tug at Dad's hand. "I think he needs ducks," I say.

Dad helps, and we unpin the ducks from over my bed and float them above his crib.

Jin Woo stretches his hand toward them and gives that nice gurgly laugh.

"He likes them," I say. "He's a happy jewel!"

I lean over the crib and laugh with him.

And I'm happy, too.